Missouri Bound

THE COMPLETE
LAURA CHAPTER BOOK COLLECTION

**Adapted from the Little House books
by Laura Ingalls Wilder
Illustrated by Renée Graef and Doris Ettlinger**

LITTLE HOUSE

Rose #1

Missouri Bound

ADAPTED FROM THE ROSE YEARS BOOKS BY

Roger Lea MacBride

ILLUSTRATED BY

Doris Ettlinger

HarperTrophy ®
A Division of HarperCollins*Publishers*

SwC
Fic
Wild
4.25

Adaptation by Heather Henson.

HarperCollins®, ®, Little House®, Harper Trophy®,
and The Rose Years™ are trademarks of HarperCollins Publishers Inc.

Missouri Bound
Text adapted from *Little House on Rocky Ridge*,
text copyright 1993 by Roger Lea MacBride.
Illustrations by Doris Ettlinger
Illustrations copyright © 1999 by Renée Graef
Copyright © 1999 by HarperCollins Publishers

Library of Congress Cataloging-in-Publication Data
MacBride, Roger Lea, 1929–
  Missouri bound / adapted from the Rose years books by Roger Lea
MacBride ; illustrated by Renée Graef. — 1st ed.
    p.   cm. — (A little house chapter book)
  "The Rose years."
  Summary: Even though she is sad to leave her home in South Dakota, Rose
has many new experiences as she and her parents and the Cooley family make
their journey to Missouri.
  ISBN 0-06-442087-6 (pbk.). — ISBN 0-06-027953-2 (lib. bdg.)
  1. Lane, Rose Wilder, 1886–1968—Juvenile fiction. [1. Lane, Rose Wilder,
1886–1968—Fiction. 2. Frontier and pioneer life—Fiction. 3. Moving,
Household—Fiction.] I. Graef, Renée, ill. II. Title. III. Series.
PZ7.M12255Mi   1999   98-54327
[Fic]—dc21   CIP
                                                                  AC

❖
First Harper Trophy edition, 1999

Contents

CHAPTER 1

Saying Good-bye

Rose Wilder was leaving the little prairie town where she had lived her whole life. She was going to drive in a wagon with her mama and papa all the way to Missouri.

Papa said there was a place in Missouri called the Land of the Big Red Apple. Mama said they were going there to start over. Farming had been hard on the South Dakota prairie. There wasn't enough rain, and the wind blew all the time. In Missouri they would have a new little farm. Maybe they would even grow apple trees.

Rose couldn't imagine leaving the prairie. She didn't want to go so far away from Grandma and Grandpa Ingalls. But she thought it might be fun to grow apples of their very own.

Every day there were things to do to get ready for the long trip. Papa and Mama told Rose that the Cooleys would be coming, too. Rose was happy. She knew Paul and George Cooley from school. Paul was two years older than Rose, and George was two years younger.

Mr. Cooley owned two big covered wagons. He had two teams of horses to pull them. Paul had told Rose that he would be driving one of the wagons.

Papa and Mama's wagon was small. They drove it mostly on Sundays.

"Can we really drive in it all the way

to Missouri, Manly?" Mama asked. Papa's name was Almanzo, but Mama had nick-named him Manly. "How will we ever fit everything in? How will we stay dry?"

"Don't worry," said Papa. "I'll figure out a way to beat the weather."

First Papa nailed wooden posts to the wagon. Then he draped a big piece of black oilcloth over the posts. He tacked the edges of the oilcloth down tight to make a roof for the wagon.

Next, Papa made oilcloth curtains. The curtains rolled up on ropes. In good weather, the curtains would stay up. In bad weather and at night, the curtains would be rolled down and tied to the wagon. When the curtains were down, the wagon became a snug little house on wheels.

Rose helped Papa paint the wagon.

They painted it black to match the curtains and the roof. When they were finished, the wagon gleamed like new.

The days before the trip went quickly. One morning, Mama told Rose it was their last day. After dinner, Rose helped Mama wash and dry the dishes. Then they packed the dishes into a wooden box. All the delicate plates and cups would stay packed until they got to their new home in Missouri. They would use tin plates and cups on the journey.

That evening Rose and Mama and Papa all took baths, even though it wasn't Saturday.

Then Rose wriggled into her best calico dress. It was red, with tiny white flowers all over it like polka dots. It had a delicate lace collar that Grandma had made last Christmas.

 4

Papa put on his Sunday suit and combed his hair and mustache. Mama wore her best dress with the white lace collar and the black shiny buttons down the front.

When they were all ready, they set out for Grandma and Grandpa's house. It was going to be their last supper together.

On the way, Papa stopped by the side of the road to pick two wild roses. "One for my little prairie Rose, who is leaving the prairie," he said, handing her a pretty pink flower.

Rose held the flower to her nose and breathed in the sweet, fresh smell.

Then Papa handed the other blossom to Mama. She smiled and let out a tiny sigh.

"What is it, Bess?" Papa asked.

Mama's real name was Laura. That's

what everyone else called her. But Papa called her Bess because Mama's middle name was Elizabeth.

"I was just thinking," Mama said. "I was a little girl when Ma and Pa brought my sisters and me here. There was no little town then. Only fields of grass, as far as you could ride."

Rose looked around. She tried to see the prairie in her mind with no town. She couldn't imagine how it had looked when Mama was her age.

When they reached Grandma and Grandpa's house, Grandma was standing at the stove. She looked as neat and tidy as she always did. Her hair was parted in the middle and pulled back into a tidy knot at the back of her head. Into the knot, Grandma had stuck her pretty shell comb.

Rose loved Grandma's comb. Every

morning, for as long as Rose could remember, Grandma had fixed her hair the same way. But now, Rose realized, she wouldn't be there to see it anymore.

Suddenly, Rose missed Grandma with all her heart, even though they hadn't left yet. She wrapped her arms around Grandma's waist and squeezed as hard as she could. Grandma's warm apron smelled

of all the good things cooking in her kitchen. Pie and bread and chicken. Rose didn't ever want to let go.

"Goodness!" Grandma said. "A bear couldn't hug any tighter."

Grandpa came in from feeding his horses. Aunt Mary stirred the gravy in the pan. Aunt Grace and Aunt Carrie set the table. The house was cozy and warm.

Grandma put platters of steaming hot food on the table. Rose looked around the table. She thought about having no more suppers at Grandma's house. Her eyes stung, and a hard lump rose in her throat.

After the dishes were washed, everyone went outside to sit on the front porch. A gentle breeze blew. The sweet smell of warm prairie grass filled the air. The only light came from the stars high above.

"Pa, would you play for us, one more

 8

time?" Mama asked.

"Why, yes, if you want me to," Grandpa said. "Run and get my fiddle, Laura."

Mama brought the fiddle and set it on Grandpa's lap. Rose could see that Grandpa's eyes were shining. His long beard was dark against the white of his shirt.

Grandpa began to play the songs he had played for Mama and her sisters when they were little girls. Rose hummed along while the grown-ups sang. She knew some of the songs from Mama's whistling and singing, but she didn't know all of them.

Finally, the fiddle sang the last tune. Mama and Papa told Rose it was time to go home to bed.

In the morning, Papa and Mama and

9

Rose got into the wagon before the sun had even come up. They drove to Grandma and Grandpa's house one more time to say good-bye.

Rose was so tired everything seemed like a dream. She hugged her aunts and Grandpa twice. She hugged Grandma three times. Then she climbed sleepily up over the wheel and onto the seat. She sat in between Mama and Papa.

The mares, Pet and May, were hitched to the wagon. Their colts, Little Pet and Prince, were only four months old. They stood beside their mothers sniffing the fresh morning air.

Papa tightened the reins and raised his hat. Everyone cried out all at once, "Good-bye! Good-bye! Don't forget to write!"

And then they were on their way.

Mama and Papa were silent as the horses pulled the wagon through the quiet little town.

When they passed the last house, they caught up with the Cooleys. Papa stopped beside one of the Cooleys' wagons. Rose saw that Paul was driving it all by himself.

"Howdy, Mr. and Mrs. Wilder," Paul shouted. George sat next to his brother. Mrs. Cooley sat next to Mr. Cooley on the other big wagon.

Papa waved and the three wagons began their long journey.

Rose wanted to stay awake, but she couldn't keep her eyes open. Mama fixed a place in the back of the wagon where she could sleep. Rose took one last look at the little town. Then she put her head down and fell fast asleep.

CHAPTER 2

The Dusty Trail

Rose opened her eyes. She could feel the hot sun on her face. She could hear voices singing.

"'Oh Su-sanna, Don't you cry for me!'" Papa's voice sang out.

And Mama's voice answered, "'I'm go-ing to Missouri, with my washpan on my knee!'"

Rose sat up and rubbed her eyes. She looked all around. The wagon trail stretched far behind them. The wind blew dust into the air. The little town was gone! Now there was only rolling prairie as far as Rose could see.

"Where are we?" she asked.

"We haven't gone far," Mama said. "Come sit with us and sing awhile."

Rose climbed over the back of the wagon seat.

Mama began to sing, and then Papa and Rose joined in. They sang some of the old songs Mama knew from when she was a little girl. Then they sang a new song Rose had just learned in school. The words didn't make any sense, but they made Rose laugh.

"Ta-ra-ra-boom-de-ay," sang Rose, "Ha-ha-ha-boom-de-ay."

As soon as they had sung the last note, Rose started to sing the silly song again from the beginning. Mama and Papa joined in.

At the end, there was a moment of silence. Mama and Papa looked at Rose as if to say, enough is enough.

But Rose couldn't resist. With a giggle she started the song over again. Mama and Papa laughed, and then they joined in, too.

All morning the mares plodded toward the brown horizon. Rose watched the wild-flowers nodding in the sunshine. She wished that Paul and George would turn around and wave to her. But she knew Mr. Cooley had told them not to play while Paul was driving.

Finally, the three wagons pulled up beside a tree. Everyone was thirsty, but there was no stream and no farm nearby to ask for water. So they drank from the water barrel tied to Paul's wagon.

Paul stood in the wagon box and

dipped water for each of them. The water was warm and it tasted stale. But Rose was too thirsty to care. She drank so greedily from her tin cup that she spilled some on her dress.

"Take your time, Rose," said Mama. "The horses have to drink, too. We can't afford to waste a drop. We don't know when we might find more."

Paul filled two wooden buckets from the water barrel. Rose and George carried them to the horses. Rose's bucket was heavy. At first it banged her shins and the water sloshed out. After that she walked very slowly to keep from spilling more.

Papa and Mr. Cooley unhitched the horses so they could rest, too. The horses lay down in the dust and rolled around on their backs. They were trying to roll off the sweat and tiredness.

Then Papa and Mr. Cooley tied the horses to the wagon wheels. They hung bags of oats on the mares' noses so they could eat. Papa also put some oats on the ground for the colts to munch. When it was gone, the colts moved off to nibble some grass.

Rose helped Mama and Mrs. Cooley unpack the dinner baskets. Grandma had made them fried chicken, hard-boiled eggs, bread and jam, and bread-and-butter pickles.

They all sat down to eat under the tree. Rose hoped she and Paul and George could play after dinner.

"It's good to sit in the shade, on the soft grass," Mama said. "I can still feel the wagon seat bumping along."

Even in the shade, Rose was hot. She was almost too hot to eat.

"How far have we gone now?" she asked.

"We're so close to home, you wouldn't guess we aren't going to turn around," Mama said.

"The horses know we aren't," Papa said. "They seem eager to keep going. I have to hold them back some, even in this heat."

"Maybe they can smell the water in Missouri," Mama said.

Papa had told Rose that there were bubbling springs and little creeks all over in the Land of the Big Red Apple. And there were trees everywhere.

Rose looked around. The tree they were sitting under was an island of green in a sea of brown grass. Dust whirled and twisted along the road. Rose couldn't imagine a land covered with trees, and with water everywhere, pouring out of little holes in the ground.

After dinner there was no time to play. They all climbed back into the wagons and started off again.

Later that afternoon, a dust storm blew up. The wind blew a thick cloud of dust over the wagons. The light dimmed. The air was so thick that Papa could not see the wagon trail.

"We'll have to wait it out!" he shouted over the roaring wind.

The wagons pulled off the trail and stopped. Mama unrolled the oilcloth curtains and tied them in place. She and Rose huddled inside the wagon with kerchiefs over their mouths.

Papa got down to calm the horses. He tied their reins to stakes and drove the stakes into the ground. When he climbed back into the wagon, he brought in a gust of hot, dusty air.

The wind snapped and grabbed at the heavy oilcloth curtains. It slammed against the wagon in great gusts.

Mama looked at the thermometer.

"It's a hundred and two degrees!" she cried. Her voice was muffled by her kerchief.

Rose's eyes itched. Her skin felt gritty, and her dress clung to her back. She could taste the dust through her kerchief. She could not be good a moment longer.

"I'm thirsty," she said.

"Don't complain, Rose," Mama said gently. "You must be a little patient, is all. What cannot be cured must be endured. Think how thirsty the poor horses must be."

Rose did not feel better, or more patient.

 20

But she knew to keep her complaints to herself after that.

Finally the dust cloud thinned. Then it disappeared. The sun shone bright in a yellow sky.

Dust was everywhere. It sat in little piles on the wagon seat. It was on every flat surface and inside every tiny seam. Rose's blue-flowered calico dress and bonnet were grimy. When she stood up, dust shook from her skirt in little puffs.

Everyone's face was lined with dust and sweat. The horses were covered with it. The chickens in their wire coop were covered, too. Their white feathers were frosted a pale brown.

They were all thirsty, but the water tasted muddy now. Only the horses drank it eagerly.

Rose was hot and itchy. She was

already tired of the dusty wagon trail. She watched the horses drink that muddy water and felt sorry for them. But she felt sorrier for herself. She wished they were already in Missouri.

CHAPTER 3

Making Camp

All afternoon, the wagons drove on through the dust and the heat. Finally, they came to a little grove of trees. Papa said it was time to make camp for the night.

There was a little house near the trees. And there was fresh water running from a spout into a long wooden bucket. Papa went to talk to the owner of the house. When he came back, he told them the owner said they could have as much water as they wanted.

"Here, Rose," Papa said, handing her a bucket. "Draw some fresh water for supper."

Rose ran and stuck her face right into the stream of water. Nothing had ever felt so good. She drank from the spout. She stopped to get her breath and then drank again. The water was sweet and icy cold. Rose was sure she could never drink enough of it.

Then she remembered Mama and the horses. Quickly, she filled the bucket and carried it carefully back to the wagons.

"Now that we're traveling, your chores will be different," Mama told Rose. "First thing each evening you must look for wood for the campfire. You should be able to find some fallen sticks and branches under those trees."

Carrying water was hard work. But

looking for wood sounded like a treasure hunt. Rose dashed under the trees. George was already there. He was dragging a nice big branch toward the Cooleys' stove.

It didn't seem fair to Rose that George had gotten a head start. But then she saw a broken branch lying on the ground. She ran to grab it. Some sticks were lying by a tree trunk. She ran and picked those up, too.

George saw Rose racing around, so he tried to grab the biggest sticks first.

Hunting for wood became a game. It felt so good to run after sitting in the wagon seat all day.

Rose tried hard to beat George to every stick. They were laughing and racing around so fast, they both tried to grab the same stick. They crashed into each other and fell to the ground. Their bundles of wood scattered all around.

"Hey, that's my stick. I saw it first!" George shouted.

"No it's not, either!" Rose shouted back. "I touched it first!"

"That's enough, Rose," Mama called out. "I'm waiting for that wood to start supper."

Then Rose and George quietly picked up the scattered wood and carried it back to where the stoves were set up.

Rose helped Mama break the sticks into smaller pieces to start the fire. Then she carefully peeled four potatoes. When she was done, Mama said she could watch Papa groom the mares.

Rose watched Papa brush the dust from Pet's back. He brushed and rubbed until her coat shone like satin.

"Can I help, Papa?" Rose asked. "Can

 26

I brush Pet, too?"

"She's a bit tall for you, Rose," Papa said. "And my brush is too big for your hand."

"Please, Papa!" Rose begged. "Just a little? I'll be careful."

Papa looked at Rose for a moment. He smiled and stroked his mustache.

"Well, I suppose Pet might like to have her chest scratched a bit. Let me see. I think I have an old corncob in here."

Papa looked into the bag where he kept the brushes. He fished out an old corncob and showed Rose what to do.

Rose was excited—and a little nervous. She had never helped Papa with the mares before.

Pet stood still while Rose gently scratched her chest with the corncob.

"You can talk to her," Papa said.

"Horses like to hear a voice. It soothes them."

Pet lowered her enormous head and gently tickled Rose's ear with her lips.

"I can't think of anything to say," Rose said with a giggle.

"Well, then sing to her," Papa told her.

So Rose started to sing "Ta-ra-ra-boom-de-ay" to Pet. Just then Little Pet poked his velvety nose in Rose's way.

 28

"Little Pet wants to be combed, too, Papa," Rose said.

"The colts aren't old enough," Papa said. "But here's a bit of carrot you can give him."

Rose remembered to hold her hand open wide so the colt wouldn't bite any fingers by mistake. Little Pet's breath was warm as it whooshed into Rose's palm. The colt's bright eyes looked shyly at Rose. Then Little Pet reached out and took the carrot. Rose heard three loud crunches, and the carrot was gone. Little Pet nuzzled Rose, looking for more.

Finally, Mama and Mrs. Cooley called suppertime. Mama and Mrs. Cooley had made pork and beans and fried potatoes. The grown-ups ate at Mama and Papa's table. Rose sat on the ground next to Paul and George with her tin plate on her lap.

Everything tasted delicious.

After the dishes were washed, Mama told Rose she could play until dark.

Rose and Paul and George explored the little grove of trees. The Cooleys' black-and-white dog, Ben, came with them.

Then Paul said they should have a race.

"First one to that fence post over there!" he shouted.

They raced each other through the grass. Paul was taller and his legs were longer. He usually won easily. But Rose knew she could beat George if she really tried. She ran hard and touched the fence-post just before he did.

"I beat you! I beat you!" she panted.

"Did not either!" George shouted. His face was red. "My foot was in front of yours. Touching doesn't count."

But Rose knew she had been faster. It was naughty, but part of her liked beating George.

Rose and Paul and George played until it was so dark they could hardly see one another. Then Mama called Rose for bedtime.

Rose climbed into the wagon and put on her nightgown. Mama had made her a little bed in front of the wagon seat. It was as cozy as a crib.

Behind Rose's little bed, Mama had made a big bed on top of the bedsprings. The bedsprings sat on top of the trunks. The trunks held all the things they wouldn't need until they got to Missouri.

Rose wriggled into her covers. Papa blew out the lantern.

The dark was full of little sounds. The night air whispered through the grass and the crickets chirped. The chickens in their wire cage rustled their feathers.

Then Rose heard a new sound. It was a high-pitched yapping and howling far off in the distance. She had never heard anything like it. Her scalp crinkled. Ben barked twice from under Paul's wagon.

"What was that?" Rose asked. "Is it wolves?"

Mama had told Rose scary stories about wolves, but Rose had never heard one or seen one herself.

"It's just coyotes," said Mama. "There are no wolves here. Go to sleep now."

Rose was tired, but she could not sleep. The coyotes began yapping and howling again. The wind slapped and tugged at the curtains. Rose huddled down in her little bed. She could feel her heart racing.

CHAPTER 4

Hardtacks for Lunch

The next morning, Papa had a surprise for Rose.

"Would you like to ride with Paul and George today?" Papa asked.

"Could I?" Rose cried.

"Yes," said Papa. "But you must be good. You musn't distract Paul from his driving, or Mr. Cooley won't allow a next time."

"Yes, Papa," Rose said, trying to sound

good. Inside she was jumping up and down with excitement.

Mr. Cooley lifted Rose up onto the seat. She settled herself down between Paul and George. The Cooleys' wagon was so much bigger than Papa's. Rose and Paul and George sat high above the ground.

"Is it hard to drive?" Rose asked Paul when they were on the trail.

"You have to hold the reins a certain way," Paul said. "Not too tight, not too loose. Want to try?"

"Could I?" Rose asked.

"Sure," said Paul. He showed her how to hold the reins.

Rose liked the feel of the warm leather in her hands. She knew she wasn't really driving. The lines still ran through Paul's hands, and she was only holding the ends. But it was fun to pretend.

 34

Rose and Paul and George talked as they drove. They talked about everything under the hot, blazing sun. They counted jackrabbits bounding away in the grass. They laughed to see road runners dashing ahead of the wagon. They watched the clouds in the sky and took turns saying what the clouds looked like. They wondered about Missouri, and whether they would go to the same school.

At noon, the wagons stopped in a grassy place by the trail.

There weren't any trees around, so Rose gathered dead grass and weeds for a fire. Mama boiled water for tea, and then she got the hardtacks out of the wagon.

Rose had never eaten hardtacks before. Hardtacks were white and round. They looked like dinner plates with tiny holes in them. Mama had made the holes

 36

with a nail. Hardtacks were like bread, but they were baked without any yeast, so they came out of the oven flat and hard.

Mama said hardtacks stayed fresh a long time, like crackers. She had baked a whole sack of flour into hardtacks before they left. As long as they had hardtacks, they would never go hungry.

Hardtacks were so hard, Papa had to smash each one into smaller pieces with a clean hammer. Mama poured hot water into Rose's cup. She showed her how to dip the pieces until they were soft enough to eat.

The piece of hardtack was soggy, but Rose was hungry and it tasted delicious.

After dinner, Mr. Cooley told Paul to come sit beside him. He told Paul that Mrs. Cooley was going to drive the other wagon for the rest of the day.

"We're coming to a river crossing," he explained. "I want those reins in experienced hands."

Paul's shoulders sagged. He shoved his hands into his pockets and kicked up dust as he walked to his father's wagon. Rose felt bad for him. Paul was a good driver. It wasn't fair.

They all climbed into the wagons and started off again along the trail.

"May I ride with Paul and George tomorrow?" Rose asked Mama and Papa. "I was good."

"You were good," said Mama. "You may ride with Paul and George, but only if Mr. Cooley says so."

"Wind's picking up," Papa said. "We may get a bit of rain."

Rose looked up. There were dark gray clouds in the distance.

 38

Soon they began to see other wagons coming from every direction. They were all heading toward the river crossing.

When they came over a hill, Rose saw a big winding river. It was wide and it curved far away in both directions. Rose had never seen so much water.

"How will we get to the other side?" she asked.

"See the ferry?" Mama said. She pointed to the middle of the river.

Rose could not see anything at first. Then she saw it. The ferry looked no bigger than a little piece of wood, or a leaf. It bobbed in the middle of that great big river.

Rose gulped. Something fluttered in her stomach. She looked at all that water and realized something. She didn't know how to swim!

CHAPTER 5

River Crossing

All afternoon, Rose and Mama and Papa inched toward the river. There was a long line of wagons waiting to cross. The ferry could only take one wagon at a time.

The sun began to sink, but the wind still blew hot as an oven. Dust and dry weeds flew past them. There were black clouds piling up in the sky.

The closer they came to the water, the more fluttery Rose felt. The river was looking wider every minute.

"What river is this, Mama?" Rose asked. "Is it the Mississippi?"

"This is the Missouri River, Rose," Mama answered.

"Is that Missouri on the other side, then?" Rose asked hopefully. "Are we there already?"

"No," Mama said with a chuckle. "The Missouri River is very long. The other side is Nebraska."

The river water was so brown, Rose could not see into it at all. Mama said the Missouri had a nickname: Big Muddy.

Finally it was the Cooleys' turn to cross the water. Rose watched from the riverbank as the little ferry tossed on the brown, foamy waves. Rose felt sick to her stomach seeing the Cooleys' wagon bob up and down. She did not want to get on that ferry.

41

"So! That's Nebraska!" Papa said. His voice was loud and hearty. He was trying to make Rose feel better.

Suddenly a big gust of wind hit their wagon. The whole wagon lifted up from the ground and into the air. Then it came down again with a BANG! Rose's teeth clacked together. The pots and pans crashed. The colts began to squeal with fright. Pet and May whinnied and pawed at the air. The chickens began to squawk.

"Here, take these!" Papa shouted. He handed the reins to Mama and jumped out of the wagon. Rose heard him hammering wooden stakes into the ground behind them.

Mama shouted to the horses over the wind. "Easy now, don't panic," she cried. "Whoa! Be still, May! Thatagirl, Pet."

Rose felt the wagon become steady

as Papa took pieces of rope and tied each corner tight to the wooden stakes.

Behind and above them, a cloud of dust rose up overhead. The sky had a strange, flat light and the wind became still again.

"That's your last sight of Dakota, Rose," Mama said. Her voice sounded so strange, Rose looked up. She was shocked. Mama's cheeks were damp with tears! Now Rose's throat ached. Her eyes burned. Before she could stop herself, she was crying, too.

Papa came back to the front of the wagon. He looked at Mama and Rose in surprise.

"Why, Bess!" he shouted over the wind. "What's the matter?"

Mama handed the reins to Papa. She shook her head and pulled out her handkerchief to wipe Rose's face. Then she dabbed her own.

43

A few large drops of rain spattered the wagon seat. The rain made dark circles on the dusty backs of the horses.

Rose sniffled and Mama put her arms around her. Rose felt better. But she was still afraid of that muddy water.

In a few minutes, the empty ferry came back across the river to pick them up. Then everything happened very quickly.

Papa pulled the wooden stakes out of the ground. Mama held the colts while Papa drove the wagon onto the ferry. The horses rolled their eyes and tossed their heads. They pranced and whinnied. They had never been on a ferry before.

"Ho, girls! Easy!" Papa shouted.

The horses' hooves clumped. The wheels rumbled onto the wooden platform of the ferry.

Rose grabbed the edge of the wagon

 44

seat. Everything was quivery and unsteady. The ferry was tilting and rocking in the water.

Rose looked behind her. The river-bank was getting smaller. Her stomach flip-flopped.

Then she looked forward at the choppy brown waves. She could hardly see the land on the other side. When she looked right and left, all she could see was muddy water.

Rose held on to the seat with all her might. The ferry was rocking back and forth. It felt like the whole wagon might rock right into the river. Rose's hands ached, but she would not let go.

Rose felt like crying again. She looked at Mama and Papa. They were calm. And so were the horses.

"If the horses can be good, so can I," Rose thought to herself.

Finally, the land rose up in front of them, and the ferry touched the shore.

Rose heard the horses' hooves clumping off the ferry deck. The wagon wheels crunched onto the riverbank.

Rose let out a sigh. She was happy to be on solid ground again. They were in Nebraska.

CHAPTER 6

Going Swimming

The three wagons traveled through Nebraska the rest of that day and all the next. But on Sunday, they stayed in one place. Mama said that even when people traveled, Sunday was a day of rest.

After breakfast, Mama and Mrs. Cooley sat together talking. Papa helped Mr. Cooley fix a broken harness strap.

Rose and Paul and George went exploring. In the field beside the wagons, they broke off some stalks of dried-out wheat and chewed the hard, nutty grains.

47

Rose had to chew a long time before the grains were soft enough to swallow.

"You could eat wheat all day and still be hungry," Paul said. "But don't swallow any of the seeds whole."

"Why not?" asked Rose.

"It might make a wheat stalk grow in your stomach," George said.

Rose tried to remember if she had swallowed any wheat grains without chewing.

"You're just teasing," she said.

"It could happen," George said in a serious voice.

"That's right," said Paul. "That's why I always spit out my watermelon seeds. Suppose you grew a watermelon in your stomach? How would you ever get rid of it?"

Rose was sure she had swallowed

a watermelon seed, at least once. She touched her stomach. It was flat. But from now on she would remember to spit out her seeds just in case.

For dinner, they ate cold beans with corn bread. When Rose finished helping with the dishes, Papa had a surprise.

"How would you kids like to go swimming?" he asked.

"Golly!" Paul shouted.

"Hooray!" yelled George.

"Swimming?" Rose asked. She thought about the Big Muddy, and she got that fluttery feeling in her stomach. But when she saw how excited Paul and George were, she decided it must be fun after all.

Mama and Mrs. Cooley and Rose put on their oldest calico dresses. Papa and Mr. Cooley wore their overalls, and so did Paul and George.

Rose raced with Paul and George ahead of the grown-ups. Clouds of grasshoppers flew through the grass as they ran. The grasshoppers landed with little patting noises that sounded like drops of rain.

The little stream was clear and glittering. It was not muddy and ugly like the Missouri River.

Rose stepped into the water. The sandy bottom was warm. The sand ran between her toes as she walked. It made her unsteady. When she stood still, the sand drifted over her feet until they were completely covered up.

Rose was standing still, looking at her feet, when all of a sudden there was water running over her head and down her face. It ran down her back and into her dress! The water was cold. The shock

 50

took her breath away.

Then she heard Paul behind her. He was laughing. He had his hat in his hands. Water was sloshing out of it.

"Golly, Rose," he shouted. "You're all wet!"

He laughed again and threw water from his hat right in Rose's face. She gasped. For an instant she didn't know what to do.

Then Rose lunged. She hit Paul in the chest with both hands. He fell back into the water.

Now Paul was soaking wet, too. He opened his mouth to speak, but nothing came out. His eyes were round. He looked so funny, Rose began to laugh.

Then they all started splashing one another, even the grown-ups. The cool water felt so good in the hot sunshine.

All afternoon, Rose and Paul and George chased one another through the shallow pools. They ran and splashed until they were out of breath. Then they sat right down in the cool, bright water.

They took turns pouring hatfuls of water over one another's heads.

When it was her turn to get wet, Rose opened her mouth and drank. She loved the feel of the cool water on her skin. She wished they could go swimming every day.

Swimming was an adventure. Even something scary—like crossing the Big Muddy—was an adventure. Rose couldn't wait to see what her next adventure might be.

CHAPTER 7

The Russians

Each day the three wagons rolled farther south toward Missouri. Each night they set up camp, and on Sundays they rested.

One Sunday, a group of Russians came to visit the campsite. Rose had never seen a Russian before.

The Russians came walking across the field in one big group. They all had friendly smiles. Their faces were pink and their hair was the color of spun gold. They were speaking words that didn't sound like words at all.

The men wore crisp blue shirts. The boys were dressed just like the men.

The women wore handkerchiefs over their heads. They all had thick braids that hung down their backs like golden ropes. Their dresses were blue to match the men's shirts. The skirts stood out stiff and thick with petticoats. The girls were dressed just like the women.

Rose couldn't stop looking at them. She thought they were beautiful. She loved the strange sound of their words.

Two Russian women stepped forward. One of them handed a basket of potatoes to Mama. The other held out a pail of fresh milk to Mrs. Cooley.

"It must be a gift," Mama said. She thanked the two women.

"*Da. Da,*" the women said.

For a moment everyone was quiet. The Russians did not know what to say. They smiled and looked around.

Finally Mama held out her hand. She showed the Russians that they were invited to stay and visit.

"Rose, run and get some grass and sticks," Mama said. "We'll heat up the stove for tea."

The Russians began to drift about the

camp. They looked at the little black wagon. They walked around it and pointed. They spoke to each other in pleasant voices. Some of the men stood admiring Papa's colts. The men nodded their heads and pointed.

One of the old men looked at the hammock that Aunt Mary had made before they went away. Papa always strung it between two wagons when they were stopped on Sundays.

"Please," Mama said, pointing to the hammock. "Won't you sit?"

The old man touched the edge of the hammock. It began to swing.

"Like this," Mama said. She sat down in the hammock and swung back and forth. Then she got up and patted the hammock again.

The old man sat down slowly. When

he was in the hammock he smiled at his friends. Then he leaned back. In one smooth motion, he flipped backward, right out of the hammock! He landed in the dust with a thud.

Everyone became silent.

Rose started to laugh inside. The old man looked so funny. He was upside down, with his shoes tangled in the netting.

Rose tried not to laugh on the outside, but she couldn't help it. Paul and George burst out laughing, too.

"Rose!" Mama scolded. But Rose could see Mama's eyes twinkling.

The old Russian man's belly began to jiggle with laughter. He coughed and said something in Russian. Then all the other Russians laughed, too.

Now all the Russians took turns sitting

in the hammock. Some of them fell out on purpose. Then everyone howled with laughter again.

The Russians had a big dog with them. The dog was taller than Rose. It had glossy brown fur and clear green eyes. Its ears stood straight up. It looked like a wolf.

"Mama, the dog is smiling at me," Rose said.

"Why, yes it is," Mama laughed.

The wolf-dog walked right over to Rose. It licked Rose's ear with its big pink tongue. Rose wrapped her arms around the dog's neck and buried her face in its soft coat.

Then Rose felt wriggling behind her. She felt two paws pushing on her back. She turned and there was another wolf-dog! But this one was a puppy, and even more beautiful.

The wolf-puppy licked Rose's face. His bright eyes looked right into Rose's eyes. Rose gave him a big hug. She fell in love with that puppy. She wanted him for her very own.

"Oh, Mama," Rose said.

Mama smiled and looked at Papa.

Rose's stomach flip-flopped. She watched Papa turn to one of the Russian men. Papa pointed to the puppy. He reached into his pocket and pulled out a coin.

The Russian looked at the puppy and then looked at Papa. He shrugged his shoulders.

So Papa pulled out another coin. He jingled the two together in his hand.

The man smiled. He opened his mouth to speak.

Just then a little Russian girl ran over.

She hugged one of the man's legs and began to cry. The Russian man put his hand gently on the little girl's head. He spoke to her in a soothing voice.

The Russian man looked at Papa and shook his head.

"I understand," Papa said, slipping the coins back in his pocket.

Rose felt herself sinking.

"I tried, Rose," Papa said. "Looks like a mighty fine dog, too. Maybe we'll find another."

Rose couldn't say anything. She felt like crying. She buried her face in the puppy's coat.

When it was time for the Russians to leave, the puppy seemed to want to stay with Rose. But then the Russian man called out. The puppy ran back to the Russian girl.

All the rest of that day, Rose thought about the puppy. She felt like the little Russian girl had taken the puppy away from her. She knew it was wrong to want something that wasn't hers, but she couldn't help it.

CHAPTER 8

The Land of the Big Red Apple

The three wagons slowly made their way through Nebraska and crossed the border into Kansas. In Kansas, everything looked the same to Rose. Day after day, from sunrise to sunset, the horses trudged along the flat, dusty trail.

Then one afternoon, the wagons drove past a tall white post. Mama turned to Rose and smiled. "We are finally in Missouri," she said brightly.

"Is this The Land of the Big Red Apple?" Rose asked.

"Not quite, but soon," Mama said. "This is the beginning of the Ozark Mountains. The Land of the Big Red Apple is in the Ozark Mountains."

Rose started to feel excited. She could tell that Mama and Papa were excited, too. Mama whistled, and Papa talked about crops with people they met along the way.

The road wasn't flat anymore. It dipped into cozy valleys. It climbed over sunny hilltops. There were trees everywhere. And there were little streams of clear, rippling water. Missouri looked just like Papa had said it would look.

Soon, the road began to go up and up. The horses worked hard, pulling the wagons. Every time the wagons came around a turn, Rose could see woods and hills stretching out below them.

The wagons began to pass big apple orchards. Rose saw children playing in front of pretty farmhouses. There were neat wooden fences lining the road. Horses trotted up to the fences, swishing their tails and watching the wagons pass.

One day the wagons came to the top of a hill. When they came around a turn, a little town sat in front of them.

"This is it," Papa said. "This is Mansfield, Missouri."

The town wasn't big, but the streets bustled with wagons and people. A train whistle blew and a thundering engine slid into the station, screeching to a stop.

"Seems to be a busy little town," Papa said.

"Yes it does," Mama answered. She was watching everything with bright eyes.

"I do believe this is where we stop, Manly."

"And where we start anew," Papa added. He reached behind Rose to squeeze Mama's hand.

Rose nestled between Mama and Papa. She could see how happy they were. She felt safe and happy, too.

The three wagons made camp at the edge of town. Rose's family and the Cooleys would live in their wagons until they found homes of their own.

Now that the journey was over, every day was like Sunday. Rose helped Mama string the hammock between two trees. Near the wagon Mama hung sheets to make a screened place for changing and for taking baths. The table and chairs were left out, next to the wagon. After breakfast Mama left the cookstove where it stood.

There was no more packing and un-packing. When Rose finished her breakfast chores, Mama said she could play.

Rose and Paul and George loved to play in the woods near the camp. They were glad to be free of the hard wagon seats. Sometimes they went to the creek to look for Indian arrowheads.

One day Rose was playing by herself at the creek. When she looked up, she saw a little dog staring at her. It had short white fur with black and tan spots. It had pointy ears that stood straight up from a pointy face.

Rose could see that the little dog was hungry. Its ribs stuck out and it looked at Rose with big, sad eyes. Its tail hung limp.

Rose and the little dog stared at each other. Then the little dog looked at the water and panted. It laid its ears back and looked from side to side.

"What's the matter?" Rose asked. "Are you thirsty? Go ahead and drink. I won't hurt you."

She dipped the palm of her hand in the water and gave herself a drink, to show the dog that it was all right.

The dog's ears pricked up. Then it began to lap up the water in the creek. But it kept its eyes on Rose.

"Stay here," Rose said to the dog. "Don't go away."

She ran to the wagon.

"Mama, could I have some corn bread, please?" she asked.

"It's almost noon," Mama answered. "Dinner will be ready soon."

"It isn't for me," Rose said.

Mama looked at Rose. "Who could it be for?" she asked.

 68

"For . . . for a little dog," Rose answered. "If we don't give it something it might starve."

"Show me this dog," said Mama.

Mama followed Rose through the woods and down to the creek. The little dog was there, lying by the water. It looked at them with sad eyes.

"The poor thing," Mama said. She put some corn bread and a tin cup of milk in front of the dog. The dog backed away. Then it sniffed at the food and nibbled the corn bread.

Mama went back to the wagon. Rose stayed and watched the dog eat every last crumb of the bread. It lapped up the milk with its dainty pink tongue. Then it gave itself a little shake and started to walk away.

"Wait!" Rose cried.

The dog turned and looked at Rose. It took three steps toward her. Rose could see it was shivering.

"I won't hurt you," Rose said.

The dog's tail twitched once. Then the dog turned and trotted off into the woods.

Rose sighed and trudged back up the hill.

Early the next morning Rose woke from a bad dream. In her dream a growling animal had been chasing her through the woods. Rose listened to the quiet morning sounds. Then all of a sudden she heard a real growl! It came from right under the wagon. She sat straight up.

"Easy there," said a man's voice.

Rose peeked through the corner of the curtain. It was Mr. Cooley. He had come to get Papa for morning chores.

Rose heard another growl.

Papa stuck his head out the other end of the wagon. "What is it, Cooley?" he asked.

"Don't you know?" Mr. Cooley said. "There's a dog under your wagon. Acts like he wants a taste of my leg."

"A dog?" Rose shouted.

Papa climbed out of the wagon to look.

"What in the world?" Papa asked.

Rose climbed down the wagon wheel and looked. There sat the hungry white dog with the black and tan spots.

"It's him, Papa!" Rose shouted. "He came back."

The dog walked over to Rose and sat down.

Rose scratched his head. The dog's dark eyes gleamed up at her in the lamp light. Rose stroked the dog's short fur. Then she gave him a hug. The dog gave

Rose's face a little lick.

"Seems like the little thing has adopted us," said Papa. "Every farm needs a good watchdog. Shall we keep him?"

"Yes!" Rose shouted. She hugged the dog again, and he wriggled in her arms. Rose could see the little dog wasn't beautiful like the Russians' wolf-dog. He was small and bony. His thin legs trembled and his eyes were sad. But Rose didn't care. There was something special about him.

"What shall we name him?" Rose asked.

"Now, what's a good name for a faithful watchdog?" Mama wondered out loud. "How about . . . Fido?"

"Fido?" Rose said. "What's a Fido?"

"That is a very old Latin word," Mama answered. "It means faithful and loyal."

"Fido," said Rose.

The little dog's ears perked up.

"Fido," Rose said again, a little louder. The dog raised his head. He looked at Rose and blinked and panted.

"He smiled at me!" Rose shouted. "He knows we are talking about him. Fido knows."

Then she said "Fido" once more, just to hear the sound of it. The dog's eyes seemed to light up. She knew that Fido was the perfect name.

Rose gave Fido another hug. Now she had a dog, and soon they would have a little farm of their very own.

Rose looked up at Mama and Papa and grinned. She was glad they had come to the Land of the Big Red Apple.